Butterfly, Butterfly

By CarrieAnne

Butterfly, butterfly, in the sky.

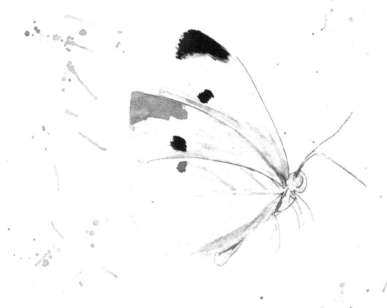

Fluttering, fluttering, oh, so high.

Where are you going?

What do you see?

Two brown flowers and a Chickadee.

Butterfly, butterfly, in the sky.

Fluttering, fluttering, oh, so high.

Where are you going?

What do you see?

Three purple flowers
and some little
snow peas.

Butterfly, butterfly, in the sky.

Fluttering, fluttering, oh, so high.

Where are you going?

What do you see?

Four yellow flowers
   by an old oak tree.

Butterfly, butterfly, in the sky.

Fluttering, fluttering, oh, so high.

Where are you going?

What do you see?

Five green flowers and a cup of tea.

Butterfly, butterfly, in the sky.

Fluttering, fluttering, oh, so high.

Where are you going?

What do you see?

Six pink flowers and a set of keys.

Butterfly,

butterfly,

in the sky.

Fluttering,

fluttering,

oh, so high.

Where are you going?

What do you see?

Seven black flowers and a little froggy.

Butterfly,
butterfly,
in the sky.

Fluttering,
fluttering,
oh, so high.

Where are you going?

What do you see?

Eight orange flowers
and a rubber ducky.

Butterfly, butterfly, in the sky.

Fluttering, fluttering, oh, so high.

Where are you going?

What do you see?

Nine white flowers down by the sea.

Butterfly, butterfly, in the sky.

Fluttering, fluttering, oh, so high.

Where are you going?

What do you see?

Ten blue flowers as happy as can be.

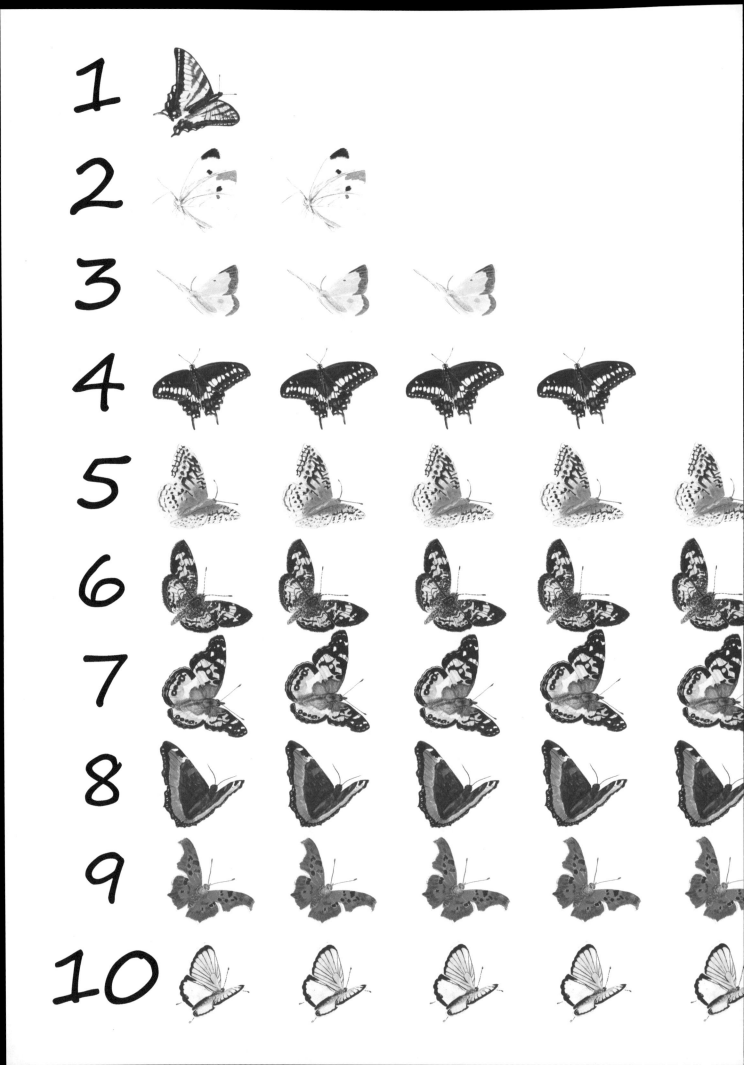

Count the Butterflies

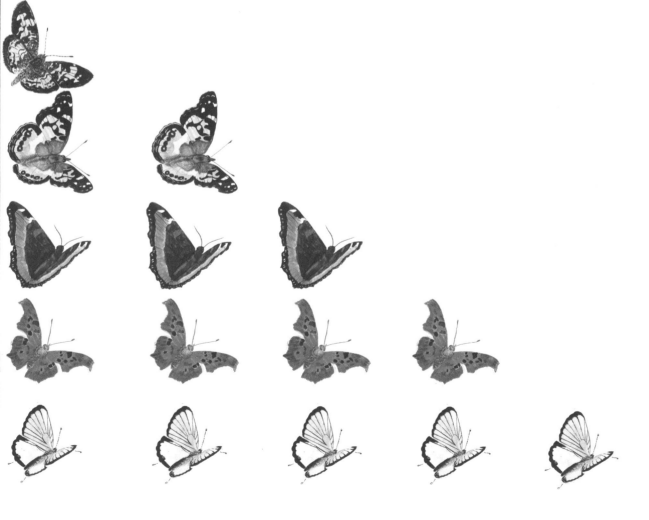

Canadian Tiger Swallowtail

Painted Lady

Milberts Tortoiseshell

American Lady

Clouded Sulphur

Eastern Tailed Blue

Black Swallowtail

Cabbage White

Question Mark

Great Spangled Fritillary

Purple Snow Pea

White Dasiy

Green Chrysanthemum

Blue Forget-Me-Not

Yellow Crocus

Orange Day Lily

Black Pansy

Pink Tuplip

Red Rose

Brown Sunflower

About the Author

CarrieAnne is a children's librarian by day, and a writer and artist by night. Inspired by a lifetime of exploring the outdoors, and her love of nature, animals and art, CarrieAnne has brought to life her first picture book. When not absorbed into the colorful world of creating, CarrieAnne enjoys camping, walking her dogs, and spending time with her family. She lives in Michigan, with her husband, daughters and too many animals to count.

Visit CarrieAnne at
www.carrieanne555.com